D1538885

NOT FOR RESALE

MOONBEAM

SELMA AND JACK
WASSERMANN

ILLUSTRATIONS
GEORGE ROHRER

BENEFIC PRESS · CHICAGO

The Moonbeam Books

MOONBEAM

MOONBEAM IS CAUGHT

MOONBEAM AND THE CAPTAIN

MOONBEAM AT THE ROCKET PORT

MOONBEAM AND THE ROCKET RIDE

MOONBEAM AND DAN STARR

MOONBEAM FINDS A MOON STONE

MOONBEAM AND SUNNY

MOONBEAM AND THE BIG JUMP

MOONBEAM IS LOST

Library of Congress
Number 67-27419

Copyright 1975, 1965 by Benefic Press
All Rights Reserved
Printed in the United States of America

CONTENTS

Moonbeam and Big Ellie

Chimps! Chimps! Chimps!

Chimps play here.

They laugh and jump and play.

5

This chimp is
Moonbeam.
She is little.
Moonbeam plays
with the chimps.

Here is Big Ellie!
Big Ellie likes the chimps.
Look out, chimps!

"BROOO!" went Big Ellie.

Up jumped the chimps.

They ran and ran!

Moonbeam laughed and laughed.

She liked Big Ellie.

Moonbeam liked to play with Big Ellie.
Big Ellie looked at Moonbeam.

"Broo!" he went.
Moonbeam jumped up on Big Ellie.

Look Out, Moonbeam!

Away went Big Ellie.

"Hoon! Hoon!" said Moonbeam.

She liked this.

Big Ellie stopped.

He liked to play here.

Down jumped Moonbeam.

In went Big Ellie.

Moonbeam looked at Big Ellie play.
She looked and laughed.
"Hoon! Hoon!" she said.

Look out, Moonbeam!

"Heen!" said Moonbeam. "Heen! Heen!"

She jumped up and ran.

Big Ellie looked at her.

"Broo?" he went.

Moonbeam ran and ran.

The little chimp ran on and on.

Look, Moonbeam!

What is it?

Moonbeam stopped.

The Truck

Moonbeam looked at the truck.

She looked at the men.

What is in the truck?

Moonbeam ran up to it.

What is this, Moonbeam?

Moonbeam looked at it.

She liked it!

"Hoon! Hoon!" she said.

The men looked at the truck.

They went up to the truck and
jumped in.

Away went the truck.
It went with Moonbeam
in it!
Moonbeam looked up.
"Hon? Hon?" she said.

Moonbeam looked out.

"Broo?" went Big Ellie.

Big Ellie looked at Moonbeam.

On went the truck.

Big Ellie looked after it.

He liked Moonbeam.

He went after the truck.

Moonbeam and the Men

The truck went on and on
with Moonbeam in it.
Moonbeam looked out.
She liked to look.

The truck stopped here.

The men jumped out.

"Here it is," they said.

The men went up to the truck and stopped.

"Look!" they said.

"This little chimp is in the truck!"

Moonbeam looked at the men.

The men looked at Moonbeam.

"Here, little chimp!"
said the men.

They liked her.

"Heen!" said Moonbeam.

Down she jumped.

"Here, little chimp!"
said the men.

Moonbeam looked
at the men and ran.

The men looked
after her.

They laughed and
laughed at her.

The Children and the Chimp

Moonbeam ran and ran.

Men stopped to look at her.

Moonbeam ran on.

The little chimp ran, and stopped.

What is in here?

Moonbeam looked at it.

She went up to it.

Moonbeam jumped
up.
She looked in.
Children and
children and
children!

Moonbeam
looked and
looked.
And in
she went!

"Look!" said the children.

"Chimp! Chimp!" they said.

They jumped and laughed.

"Here, chimp!" they said.

Moonbeam ran.

Up and down she ran.

The children jumped up and
ran after her.

Moonbeam looked at the children.

She ran out.

The children ran out after her.

"Stop the Chimp!"

Moonbeam ran.

The children ran after her.

Men laughed.

"Look at this!" they said.

What is this,
Moonbeam?
Moonbeam
stopped to look
at it.

She went in.

Look at this, Moonbeam!
The little chimp looked.
She liked it.
And she ran out with it!

Moonbeam ran on.

"Stop the chimp!"
men said.

They ran after her.

Moonbeam ran in here.

Moonbeam ran out.

Look at her!

The little chimp ran

on and on.

She went in here.

Moonbeam jumped up.

Moonbeam jumped down.

Men jumped after her.

Moonbeam ran out.

The men ran after her.

"Stop the chimp! Stop her!"
they said.

Moonbeam ran and ran.

Men ran after her.

Children ran after her.

Here Is Big Ellie!

Moonbeam ran here and stopped.

She looked at the men.

She looked at the children,

"Heeeen!" she said. "Heeen! Heeen!"

"BROOOOO!"

It is Big Ellie!

The men and children

looked at Big Ellie.

They jumped up and ran.

Moonbeam laughed.

She jumped up on Big Ellie.

And away they went.

Look! The chimps!
The chimps looked at Moonbeam.
They laughed and laughed at her.
Big Ellie looked at the chimps.
Look out, chimps!

The chimps stopped laughing.
They jumped up and ran.

"Hoon! Hoon!" laughed Moonbeam.

"Broo!" went Big Ellie. "Broo!
Broo!"

Away went Big Ellie and the
little chimp.

VOCABULARY

The total vocabulary of this book is 35 words, excluding proper names and sound words. The 25 words in roman type should be familiar to children reading on a pre-primer level. The 10 words above pre-primer level are shown in italic type. The numbers indicate the pages on which the words first appear.

after 22
and 5
at 9
away 10

Children 28
chimp 5

down 11

he 9
her 14
here 5

in 11
is 6

it 15

jump 5

laugh 5
like 7
little 6
Look 7

men 16

on 9
out 7

play 5

ran 8

said 10
She 6
stop 11

the 6
They 5
This 6
to 9
truck 16

up 8

went 8
what 15
with 6